Perfect Joy

Stephanie Perry Moore

MOODY PUBLISHERS
CHICAGO

© 2006 by
STEPHANIE PERRY MOORE

Editor: Tanya Harper
Cover Design: Jaxon Communications
Interior Design: Ragont Design

ISBN-13: 978-0-7394-8018-2

Printed in the United States of America

For
Kimberly Brickhouse Monroe
and
Joy Barksdale Nixon
(two of my dearest middle school girlfriends)

It's amazing you both have daughters who read my books.
Seems like only yesterday we were all cheering
at Matoaca Middle School ourselves.
Looking back on those memories, I'm filled with joy.
I pray the rest of your lives and every reader's life is perfect in Him!

Contents

Acknowledgments

I should be on top of the world. God has blessed my family so we could move into a brand new home. He's softened the hearts of publishers to offer me contracts on some of my other ideas. And the Lord has allowed me to see the impact of my writing as I'm interacting a lot with readers since I'm speaking more. However, my life is far from perfect and some days I have no joy. Tired of not being satisfied, I prayed, *Lord help me find the key to staying upbeat.*

Then God revealed to me that even though I don't like unpacking boxes, I have to work extra hard to meet deadlines, and I find traveling from home isn't always easy, it's okay to let out my frustrations. The Lord wants you and me to bring all our burdens

to Him, so we won't have to carry the heavy loads anymore. See, our lives will have trials, but as long as we
keep focused on God He will help us see the good in
everything. I'm thankful that God sends me plenty of an-
gels on earth to help me maintain peace.

For my parents, Dr. Franklin and Shirley Perry, Sr.,
thanks for always being there. So good to count on you.
Your consistency is a blessing.

For my publisher, Moody/Lift Every Voice, and all the
bookstore folks that push these books. I'm thankful we're
partnering together to bless many. Your support makes
me feel good.

For my fellow Flat Shoals Elementary Board members, thanks for truly making my year as president a good
one for the school. Because of your hard work I didn't
have to do everything and was able to meet my deadlines.
Your support allowed me to exhale.

For my adorable girls, Syndi and Sheldyn, I know it
seems Mom makes your life less than perfect when I say
No. But keep smiling—sometimes I do say Yes. Know I
do everything because I love you.

For my husband, Derrick, thanks for twelve years.
Not always perfect times, but every moment treasured.
Thinking of our future together brings me joy.

For my sweet, preteen readers, thanks for wanting to
learn something through taking in the words in these
pages. Remember God can handle anything. I pray this
story makes your day.

And for my Savior, thanks for all my many blessings. My heart takes excellent pleasure in writing for You. Your love makes me smile.

1

Flawless Jewel

Wow," I said, looking into the mirror on the first day of school. "I look good. I can't wait until everybody sees me." I couldn't believe I was in sixth grade. Good-bye, elementary school. Carmen Browne was headed to middle school. I loved my look. I had on a slammin' new outfit, and my hair was in dope spiral curls, shaking from side to side every time I moved my head. Though I liked my look on the outside, I was even more pumped about my inner self.

Being a Christian, I knew that I truly had it going on. Not because of me, but because the Holy Spirit lived inside of me, and He is da' bomb.

The morning went smoothly, my sister Cassie didn't give me any problems, and my brother Clay wasn't trippin'. He was actually very cool.

"I'ma show you around, sis, when we get to school," Clay told me as he gobbled down his pancakes.

Even though I'd gone to orientation a week before, I was still nervous about being late for class. But with Clay's help I wasn't sweatin' anything.

I devoured the pancakes, extra crispy bacon, and eggs with cheese that my mom cooked for us. They were delicious. After finishing breakfast, brushing my teeth, and getting my lunch money, I put on my new, hot pink backpack and headed to the door to catch my bus. My mom was dropping Cassie at school, and Clay and I would ride the bus.

"Let your dad give you a ride this morning, princess," my father said as he gave me a kiss on the cheek.

"Yeah, Carmen, let's catch a ride with Dad. I'll even let you sit in the front," Clay said.

Though I was growing up, I knew my dad still considered me as his little girl. Actually, getting a ride with him made me smile.

I didn't know why my dad started lecturing me about what he expected of me. Now I understood why Clay gladly took the backseat, and I didn't feel so privileged anymore. Then I thought about it. My dad cared about his oldest daughter, and he wanted me to know that he expected me to make him proud.

"I'm not sending you to school to socialize, nor is this fashion-show time. You're not there to be popular. I'm sending you to Matoaca Middle School to get a good education. Understand?"

As we pulled up to the parking lot, I said, "I hear you Dad. I got you." I waved at him, jumped out of the car, and rushed to catch up with my friends. Clay had already taken off.

It was hard to find Layah and Riana. I turned around and looked at the car and noticed my dad was still in the parking lot. I guess he wanted to watch me to make sure I was okay. I had to make him proud.

Lord, I prayed silently, *I'm nervous. Please be with me and help my dad know that You've got me.*

"There you are!" Layah said, running into me.

"Oww," I said as she grabbed my arm and interrupted my prayer.

Layah backed away. "Sorry, I don't want to mess up your gear. I got you, Miss Pretty; let me step to the side."

"It's nothing like that, Layah, you hurt my arm," I said as I inched closer to her.

"Yeah, right, you just too cute today and don't wanna get dirty."

"That's not true," I told her. "You seen Riana?"

"Yeah, she's over there, mad at you," Layah said as she pointed at Riana.

Layah and I started walking toward Riana. I couldn't believe that my friend would be mad at me for any reason.

This was our first day of middle school. Things were supposed to be perfect. I looked at Layah, perplexed. My tough girlfriend knew she needed to tell me why Riana had issues with me.

"She said that you were too good to ride the bus this morning, and that you should have at least told her so she could have ridden with you." Layah then nodded her head after giving me the 411, like she was on Riana's side.

Setting her straight, I said, "In the first place, I didn't even know that my dad was giving me a ride. He lectured me about how to act in middle school, so trust me, she wouldn't have wanted to ride in my car anyway."

When Layah and I walked up to Riana, before I could even give her a hug and explain that I didn't mean to make her feel bad, Clay walked up to us. He had some of his eighth grade classmates with him. They happened to all be girls.

"Oh, your little sister looks so cute," one of them said to Clay.

The other girls had similar responses. I thought my friends and I giggled a lot. These girls had us beat. I was feeling good again and wanted to introduce the girls to my friends. But when I turned around, Layah and Riana were gone. So I kept talking to the eighth graders.

The bell rang for us to enter the building. Since my two buddies were gone, I walked in with my brother's crowd. Though I hated that I couldn't find Layah and Riana, it felt good "rolling with the big dogs," as my brother would sometimes say. I had no idea how popular Clay was. Everywhere we walked someone else spoke to us. I loved the hype. I guess with him being the school quarterback, and a kinda cute guy, I should have expected it.

When I went down the sixth grade hall to find my locker, I was excited when I saw Layah and Riana.

"Hey y'all!"

"Oh, now you got time for us," Layah said angrily.

"Why are y'all trippin'?" I asked Layah.

Layah rolled her eyes and turned her back to me.

I looked at Riana and said, "I know you're not still mad, right?"

She quickly turned her back to me too, and started fiddling with her combination lock. I felt so frustrated; steam was practically coming out of my ears. *How dare they be mad at me,* I thought. *I looked for them; they left me, so I hung out with Clay and the other eighth graders. What in the world was the big deal?*

Breaking it down, I said, "What's really the problem? That I was getting compliments and hanging with eighth graders? Are you mad because I didn't catch up with you guys until now? If you're my friends you can't be jealous of petty stuff."

Riana looked away. Layah had a smirk on her face, like nothing I said made sense to her. I didn't care though. They were gonna hear what I had to say.

I continued, "I don't want to feel like you guys are going to get mad because I'm talking to other people or you feel like I'm not paying attention to you. I don't want friends like that."

I didn't know how they would take it. Part of me wanted to take my strong words back. However, I'd said it already, and I meant it. I tried to open my locker and had a hard time with the combination. I tried about five times before I finally got it open, put some books inside, slammed it really hard, and left the two of them standing there looking silly.

Yeah, they were my friends and I loved them a lot, but they were just hatin'. This summer we'd just learned what true friendship really was. I held my head high and went on to my first class, English. I thought to myself, *They are not going to ruin Carmen Browne's first day!*

✪

Thankfully, the next day I didn't have to go to school, because it was Saturday. It was the first home game for my dad's Virginia State Trojans team. My whole family was really excited. My dad and his team had worked hard all summer. He said that his team was ready with football fundamentals and mentally up for the challenge to win as well. Sitting in the president's box, we awaited game time.

I prayed silently, *Lord, please let my father stay calm, give him strength to be the best head coach Virginia State has ever had, and if it's Your will, let them win. In Jesus' name. Amen.*

From the opening kickoff, we were all on our feet. The Trojans ran for a touchdown. My dad's team was so dominant.

"I don't see your boyfriend," Cassie teased. I punched her lightly on the arm, and pretended like what she said didn't matter to me at all. Like, who cared where Spencer Webb was. Spencer, or "Spence," as we called him, wasn't at school on the first day, or at least I didn't see him. Actually I looked really cute and I would have loved for him to have seen me. I needed to quit telling myself that it really didn't bother me when it did. He wasn't my boyfriend or anything like that, but sometimes I caught myself thinking about him . . . wondering what he was doing.

After eating some delicious buffalo wings, I put my plate down and decided to look for him. When I spotted him, he was on the football field, talking to Clay.

When the second half of the game started, Clay and Spence didn't stop talking to each other. "Uuhhh," I said in frustration.

Clay was my brother, and I was jealous of him kickin' it with my friend Spence. I didn't know why I felt that way. Sadly, I wanted it to be me having fun with Spence, not Clay, but that wasn't how it was, and that really bothered me. I couldn't enjoy the rest of the game. It seemed that even the food didn't taste good anymore. I was just miserable and all because I was envious.

Later, when we went home, Clay came into my room all excited about the game. The Trojans had beaten the other team, thirty-five to zero. My excitement was gone.

"Did you see that game, man; Dad's quarterback was flawless. I sure hope I can throw like that this year."

I didn't look over at my brother. I didn't smile. I didn't even respond, and finally he got the point that he was getting on my nerves.

"What's wrong with you?" he asked, irritated.

Again he got no response from me. I was mad at him. He needed to figure out what was wrong with me or leave me alone until I was over it. He took the pillow from my bed and swatted me with it. Usually I'd grab the other pillow and we'd have a knock-down, drag-out pillow fight, but not this time.

Clay quickly got my attention. "See, I was just about to tell you that your boy Spence asked about you today, but, nope, you're acting all crazy. Bye."

"Clay, wait! I can't imagine him saying anything about me. You hogged all his time today. He's my friend and I didn't get to talk to him at all. I'm sure thinking about me was the last thing on his mind since he had you to hang out with."

"Oh, so that's what this is all about—you act like nobody can talk to lil' Spence but you. It's like that, huh? C'mon, sis. I'm keeping an eye on the dude that thinks my sister is cool. That's why I started hanging out with him in the first place. Now I like him. He's all right. You don't have to be jealous when you think I got something you don't have. I've been trying to introduce you to the older girls to make you a little popular. I hooked you up yesterday. I'm sort of doin' the same thing with Spence. Hangin' out with an eighth grader makes him look good. Believe that. But you need to check yourself. I have to look out for you because you don't know what's up."

He didn't give me a chance to respond; he just turned and walked out. I sat there, picked up the pillow he dropped on the floor, and rocked back and forth, thinking, *I can't be jealous of Clay. He's right; it's just not cool.* I needed to get it together.

I was the first one to get ready for church the next day. It didn't matter what I put on; it wasn't about how I looked. It was about needing to hear something to make me better. My mom told me how proud she was of me, because I was taking my Christian walk seriously. And though I was excited about going to church, I knew I didn't deserve any praise.

Maybe I'd been a little harsh on my friends. When they became jealous of me, or felt insecure about the attention I got, was the same thing I felt the very next day when my brother was getting attention from someone I wanted to notice me. How could I not put myself in my buddies' shoes?

My pastor, Reverend Wright, was so on point with his message. He preached a sermon about the sisters Mary and Martha. He told us that Jesus was coming to visit them. Martha had been working all day to get the house ready for Jesus. Mary, on the other hand, sat at Jesus' feet and listened to His every word. Sister Martha got really jealous that Jesus seemed to appreciate Mary's attention to Him. Reverend Wright said Jesus told Martha that she couldn't be mad at what her sister did for Him. Reverend Wright said that all of us are susceptible to envy and jealousy so we need to guard our hearts.

He preached, "We only see our own needs. We only see our own wants and we get confused. It's a daily struggle that we need to bring before the Lord. Martha had to realize that, yes, she had done a lot, but her sister had done the most important thing by just giving Jesus her undivided attention. Though Martha thought Mary's job wasn't important, to Jesus it was very important."

What a good lesson for me to learn. Life wasn't just about me. In order to please God, I had to care about others' feelings. But knowing that and doing it were two different things.

Reverend Wright continued and gave me the direction I needed. "When you become jealous of someone, just take it to Jesus. Tell Him, 'Thank You Lord,' for what He's given you, and learn how to rejoice when others rejoice. That's loving your neighbor as yourself."

Riding home, I thought about what Reverend Wright said. I didn't know why I acted the way I did sometimes, but he told us how to work on it. I wasn't going to be a perfect Christian. After all, I wasn't the King of Kings or Lord of Lords, but I would certainly strive to be a flawless jewel.

2
With imperfections

I had only been in school for two weeks and things weren't going so great. Yeah, I was still sort of popular, as popular as any sixth grader could be. I was cool with Clay's eighth grade friends, but I really missed my own friends.

Layah and Riana hadn't spoken to me since the first day in the hall when I left the two of them. And since we didn't have any classes together, or didn't speak at lunch-time, my connection with them was very distant. I asked my Social Studies teacher if I could be excused to go to the restroom and was surprised when I saw the two of them in there. They were huddled together. I wondered what they were talking about. I was so excited to see them.

"Hey, y'all!" I said excitedly. When they looked up at me, I saw Layah's eyes filled with tears.

"What do you want?" Layah snapped, sadness in her voice.

"What's wrong, Layah? Riana, what's going on with her?"

Though I asked with deep concern, I don't think they wanted me in on their conversation. But I couldn't just turn and walk away. I couldn't leave my friend in tears. I had to stay. In my head, Layah was my girl for life.

"Tell me what's wrong."

Layah pushed herself up from the corner, got all up in my face, and said in a mean way, "My grandmother has cancer and is in the hospital, fighting for her life. She might not make it. Okay! There, you happy? Now you know."

Layah wasn't the only one crying at that point. My eyes began to water as she quickly dashed out of the bathroom and Riana followed her, leaving me alone. All of this was so hard to take. Even though my friends weren't treating me right, I was still sad for Layah.

What in the world was cancer anyway? Why was it so devastating? All I knew was that it was a bad disease. I wanted more information. Until then I just asked God for a miracle.

I prayed a quick prayer. *Lord, please heal Layah's*

grandmother. Layah is scared of losing her, and I don't want my friend to feel that pain. Amen.

☀

Soon I was home and not in a good mood. Clay and Cassie quickly left me alone with my attitude. I didn't even want the snack my mom had fixed for me.

She came into my room and asked, "Young lady, why are you slamming doors around here? What's going on, Carmen? Talk."

The tears flowed again, faster than a waterfall. I was overcome with emotion. At that point I felt no sixth grader in the world had a tougher start in school than me.

"Sweetheart," she said as she sat on my bed with her arms outstretched toward me. "Talk to me."

"It's so much, Mom. Life is so messed up. Now it's Layah's grandmother. She might die."

"What?" my mom asked me with a puzzled look on her face.

"Well, I don't know for sure, Mom, if she's going to die or whatever, but her breast cancer is worse. Layah told me today and she was really upset. Mom, what is cancer? Why does it mess people up so bad?"

My mom told me there are different kinds of cancers. She said, "In every body, our cells divide and grow in a controlled manner. But sometimes cells grow and divide wildly."

"Is that cancer?" I asked. "When cells grow too fast?"

"Cells can grow a mass of tissue," Mom told me. "These can be called lesions or tumors. But not all tumors are cancerous."

"They're not?" I asked.

"Some tumors are what we call *benign*. That means they're not cancerous, and they can often be removed by surgery and usually won't come back. But the word for cancerous tumors is *malignant*."

"Then what happens?"

"Malignant tumors can travel to other parts of the body. That's what it means when you hear that someone's cancer has spread."

Mom explained that in most cases the cause of a cancer is unknown, but some people have certain risk factors that seem to make them more likely to develop it. She also told me that there is no typical way to feel when a person learns that they have cancer. Everyone feels and responds in different ways. People experience different emotions—ranging from being scared, sad, mad, to being motivated to beat it. She said it's best to learn as much as possible about cancer and treatment options so that the person can pursue what is best for her.

To encourage me Mom said, "But don't sulk and cry, Carmen. I want Layah's grandma to be well too. We're going to trust God for the outcome. We believe that His will is what's best for us. Also, I want you to remember that this earth is not our home. We're traveling through here and we can't get to heaven if we don't die. And I certainly want to go to heaven, don't you?"

"Yeah, Mom, I do, and because my life is so messed up I wish I was there now, so things would be perfect," I said honestly.

She giggled. "Some days I feel the same way, baby, but God wants us to be content with where we are. Life will get better. Hold on. This life will never be 100 percent perfect, but remember God is always with you, even now. He can make you have joy. So you're covered."

Later on that night, my mom came into my room again. "Are you feeling better, sweetie?" she asked as she tucked me into bed.

"Oh, Mom," I said in despair, "middle school is so hard."

"Baby, earlier when you told me how messed up your life felt, I couldn't get it out of my mind. I wanted to give you some space, and see if you would come and talk to me. I thought maybe there was something else going on besides the situation with Layah's grandmother. I don't want my daughter going to bed feeling like stuff is too hard to bear. You've got God. You have Dad and me. What else is going on?"

I told my mom how my two best friends in the whole world, Layah and Riana, were mad at me, even though we

vowed over the summer not to let anything come between us. My heart was broken into a million pieces because they refused to talk to me.

"Why are they mad at you?" my mom asked, stroking
my hair.

"I'm popular."

"You're popular? Stop! Tell me about it."

"It's not a good thing. I mean, I was excited at first because everybody liked me. Clay hooked me up, Mom. All
the older girls talk to me. They think I wear really cute
clothes. It's not like Layah and Riana don't have cute
school clothes, but for some reason I've been getting all of
the attention. How am I supposed to deal with that,
Mom? How can I get my friends back?"

As always, she asked me tough questions, like did I
rub their noses in the fact that I had new clothes. Maybe I
did. However, that wasn't what I meant to do. Plus, I had
apologized a lot for that in the last couple of weeks. But
none of that made any difference with the two of them.
"They decided not to like me and that's just been that," I
explained.

"I know it hurts, baby, but all you can do is pray.
They're your best friends. They'll come around. Just keep
praying, being open, and willing to give them the grace
that you thought they didn't give you. Show them what
true friendship is by hanging in there."

"Yeah, okay, Mom, I'm always showing them what real
friendship is. What did they ever do for me?"

"That's just it. Friends shouldn't have to do anything to prove their worthiness to gain favor with you. And if I recall correctly, I remember you begging Riana to forgive you last year when we first moved here. You treated her badly and she forgave you. And you already said Layah's going through a tough time with her grandmother not doing well. Cut them both some slack. You're a big girl. You're in sixth grade. Be your own best friend. Remember, you're never alone; the Holy Spirit's with you."

The next day of school Mom's advice worked. I didn't need anyone. I was content with God. The day after that it worked a little less. By the third day it didn't work at all. When I saw Layah and Riana huddled together talking and then turning the other way when they saw me, it was just too much to take. I went into fourth period with my head down. That was the class that Spence and I had together.

He came up to me and said, "What's wrong with you?"

"You're a boy. You wouldn't care. You wouldn't understand."

"Yeah, boys don't stress like you girls do, but you're my friend. What's up?"

Because we had a substitute teacher, it was easy for us to pair up and talk when we got our assignments. I didn't want to tell him what was really hurting me, but because he kept asking me in a way that made me think he really cared, I finally told him that Layah and Riana had cut me out of the friendship.

"So get other friends," he said, like it wasn't a big deal. That was an excellent idea. Why hadn't I thought of that? Wow, boys could make sense sometimes.

✦

I guess I had high standards because I searched for almost a week for candidates worthy of being my friends, all the while hoping Layah and Riana would come around and let me back in the circle. When that didn't happen, I knew I had to find somebody else. I had a lot to offer, but how could I be so popular and so alone at the same time? This wasn't going to be easy.

In second period there was this girl, Christina. She was tough and she reminded me of Layah. And I thought, *Hmm, here is somebody.* But when we had a pop quiz and she asked to cheat off my test, I knew being friends with her was the last thing I needed to do.

I eased out of it by saying, "I didn't study so I wouldn't want to mess you up and give you the wrong answers. Anyway, Christina, I don't cheat."

"Oh, so you too good to do stuff like that, huh? Fine."

Lord, I thought to myself, *please help me find a good friend.*

In fifth period there was a shy girl who seemed sort of sweet. She reminded me of Riana. She told me that she liked my shirt. Maybe she was the one. Her name was Shasta. But when class was over and we walked down the hall, I knew she wasn't going to work out either. She got so nervous she had to walk behind me. Shasta didn't want anyone to laugh at her; I realized she was too paranoid, and I didn't want to get involved with someone more insecure than me.

I didn't know how to tell her we couldn't be friends, but I knew God would give me the words to say to her, if she still wanted to hang with me.

✪

The next day at lunch I didn't know where I was going to sit. I was tired of sitting all by myself. I just had to go for it, and trust that there was someone else in the sixth grade who could be my friend.

I noticed a girl sitting by herself. She sort of looked familiar, and then I realized that I recognized her. She was in a couple of my classes.

"Anyone sitting here?" I asked.

"No," she responded in a friendly tone. "Your name is Carmen, right?"

"Yeah," I said, puzzled.

"We have third and fourth period together. I'm good with names."

"Oh, yeah, I've seen you before, but I'm sorry; I don't know your name."

"No problem. I'm Imani Bastien."

"Bass-teen?"

"Yeah, that's how you say it. I'm from New York. I moved to Virginia last year with my mom. I didn't make many friends in fifth grade. So I'm sitting here alone."

"I know how you feel. I moved here last year too. I have some friends, but we don't have any classes together. I usually sit alone, so thanks."

Imani and I had a lot in common. We both were new to Virginia, and she wanted to be a journalist and I loved writing too. Both of us loved music and, most of all, were in search of a good friend. I wasn't sure if I'd like her as much as Layah or Riana, but I felt like she was the new buddy I'd asked God for.

I couldn't expect someone perfect. That wasn't realistic. I wasn't perfect and like my mom always said, "Carmen, if you want a perfect friend then be one, and since that's impossible, don't expect someone else to be."

So I had to appreciate people, even with imperfections.

3
Messed Up

"What do you mean, we have a test to-day?" I asked my new friend Imani, upset as we entered fourth period.

"It's Wednesday. Who gives a test on a Wednesday?" I asked, protesting—wanting to pull my hair out over the fact that I hadn't studied.

Science wasn't my favorite subject, but I didn't hate it either. If I had just studied a little bit, I would have been able to at least wing it on the test. This wasn't like me. I had been in school for weeks, and other than a few homework assignments, I hadn't really done much of anything.

"Miss Moss," I said, looking at my teacher. "Is this an open-book test?"

"Carmen Browne, I can't believe a bright student like you would ask me that. Stop playing around, dear. You always ask great questions in class, and your homework is excellent . . . when you do it. I hope you're prepared," she said as she turned me around, patted me on the back, and sort of pushed me back toward my seat.

I looked around the room and spotted Spence, who looked so relaxed and eager to take the test. I envied that look. I was far from excited about taking a test I wasn't ready for. I didn't know any more about molecules than I did when we started the chapter last week.

Cheating wasn't in my blood, even though Imani sat in front of me, and I could sort of see over her shoulders. I wasn't planning on going there. I couldn't. Even if the teacher didn't catch me, I knew God could see and I just didn't want to let Him down.

However, as I looked at question 1 and knew I couldn't answer it, I prayed that I could answer number 2. Unfortunately it wasn't until I got to question number 20, which was a true or false, that I even had an inkling of what the answer could be. I was in trouble. When I handed in the paper, I knew I had failed.

As I handed it in, Miss Moss smiled and said, "I hope you did well, Carmen."

I couldn't even fix my lips to smile back. Nor did I want her to grade the paper.

Imani and Spence handed Miss Moss their papers, look-ing really proud. I couldn't be upset with them. They had done what they were supposed to do, study for the test. Although I didn't know how well they did, I believed their grades were better than mine. This wasn't good. It looked like I had flunked my first test. Boy, had I messed up.

○

With my head down, I walked down the hall, knowing that I had just bombed on the test. Imani ran up behind me and surprised me, which made me drop my books onto the floor. Before I could pick them up, Spence appeared and picked them up for me.

Imani hit me in the arm and said, "Oooh, girl! Somebody likes you."

I just rolled my eyes. Who cared about boys or popularity or anything else at a time like this? I didn't even care that I should be embarrassed that my books were in everyone's way. None of that mattered. I had been in such a down mood that I hadn't even been taking care of business when it came to getting my schoolwork done. What would my parents say when they found out about my grades? Science wasn't the only class I had been slipping in. I had to get myself together.

Spence handed me my three books and whispered in my ear, "Don't worry about the test. Ace the next one. Smile."

I had to smile then. How did he know what was going on with me? I hadn't told anyone.

I gave him a really weird look and he said, "I just know you," and quickly walked away.

Imani and I shared a giggle. Spence had given me my first smile of the day. I guess boys weren't so bad when they knew how to act.

Imani and I started walking down the hall, and I saw Riana and Layah walking toward us. I had been trying to avoid them at school since they weren't giving me the time of day. I was upset about the science test, but Spence had cheered me up. And I wasn't about to let them steal my joy. So Imani and I walked right past them as if they didn't even exist.

However, I hadn't gotten very far when I heard Layah say, "Carmen Browne, can we see you for a second, please?"

She said it as if I had done something to her. I started to keep on walking, but I decided to give those two ladies a piece of my mind. They were trippin'.

"Do you know those girls?" Imani asked me.

"Yeah, just give me a second, okay?"

Going over to my two old buddies, I said, "What?"

I had absolutely no energy or excitement in my voice whatsoever. Being their friend had drained me. What did they want?

"Don't get all evil with us," Riana said. "We just wanted to say hi. You just saw us in the hall and didn't say anything. You were all into your new friend, I guess. You don't even want to give us the time of day."

"Please don't act like you're jealous," I said to the two of them. "Y'all have been walking past me for the last month. It didn't seem like it made a difference. Now when you see me walking with someone else, you want me to speak. Please. Bye, y'all."

Before I knew it Layah grabbed my arm. "Wait, okay? We have been a little rude to you. We have been a little mean."

"What? A little?" I said, alluding to the fact that she had to be joking.

"What can we do to fix it? We want things between us to be better. We miss you."

Taking a deep breath, I started to think more rationally. I was so mad at the two of them. I could have gone on and on being mad at them forever, but now they wanted things to change. They were my girls. I loved them, and here was my chance to make sure things got worked out for good.

"I'll call you guys later, okay? I miss y'all too."

Imani, obviously irritated, shouted, "The bell is about to ring."

I waved good-bye to them and caught up to Imani. I put my arm up under hers as we ran down the hall, hoping to make it to our next class before the bell rang. Thankfully we were successful. I didn't ask her why she seemed tired of waiting on me while I talked to my friends. I just assumed it was because we were almost late for class. However, I made a note to myself that Imani seemed a little clingy.

I thought about my talk with Riana and Layah for a couple of days, praying on how I would approach them. I wanted to be cautious. I didn't want any more drama.

Later that evening, Imani and I were talking about nothing on the phone when my mom entered my room and said, "All right, Miss Lady. It's time to go to bed. Tell Riana or Layah I said good night."

"Imani, I've got to go," I told her. "I'll see you tomorrow."

When I hung up the phone, my mom came over to my bed and said, "Imani? You have a new friend?"

I explained the whole situation to my mom about what was going on. I loved being able to talk to her and get good advice on how to handle things. My mom was my girl.

"You remember the old Girl Scout saying, 'Make new friends, but keep the old. One is silver, the other is gold'? Seems like you've been down about your friends not talking to you, and now they want to talk to you again. You can't ignore that. It's also okay that you have a new friend. Maybe you can have a slumber party so that Layah and Riana can get to know Imani."

"This Friday night?" I asked, excitedly jumping onto her lap.

"Yeah, that works. Your dad's got an away game. I'm not going but Clay is, and Cassie is spending the night with Riana's little sister."

I moved off her because I knew I was heavy, but threw my arms around her neck. "Oh, thanks, Mom! Thanks!"

My mom got up and walked toward the door, turned around, and said, "You're welcome, sweetie. All right, it's time for bed. Remember to put the phone back in its place on the hall table where it belongs before you get too comfortable. Say your prayers. Good night, baby."

Lately things in my life had been upside down; maybe now they were finally going to turn right side up. I sure hoped so. I just had to wait it out and see. I was ready to hold on for the ride, and with my friends, hopefully it would be a smooth one.

✪

The next morning I got up extra early to design my invitations on the computer.

You are cordially invited to a Sleepover Tea
Given by Miss Carmen Browne

Invitees:
Imani Bastien
Riana Clark
Layah Golf

Theme: Expanding our Friendship Circle
When: Friday Evening @ 7:00 PM
Place: Browne Home

Looking at the invitations, I was really pleased with myself. Then I thought to myself, *How come I'm not doing this for my schoolwork?* I just wasn't motivated enough to hit the schoolbooks, but the social girl in me was ready to throw a monster jam.

All of my friends accepted. Imani's mom came over to meet my mom about 5:30, since we were new friends and she was spending the night at my house. It turns out my mom and Imani's mom had met at our school's open house back in the summer. Layah and Riana arrived at 7:00 exactly. My three friends said hello to one another, and from that point they never agreed on anything else. Layah and Riana wanted to do one thing and Imani wanted to do something else. It was hard for me because the something else that Imani wanted to do was actually what I wanted to do as well. Finally, someone who saw things my way. A good movie and popcorn—yes! No Barbie dolls, no Xbox; this was girl time.

"We're your guests, Carmen. You should do what we want to do," Layah said.

"Yeah, but you're in her home," Imani stepped up to them and challenged. "She sets the rules and the plan; we just follow. You accepted the invitation."

"Hey, guys," I stepped in between the two of them and said. "I don't want us to argue."

"Girls," my mom called out from the top of the stairs. "You guys come on up and get some tea."

The aroma of chamomile brew and homemade

gingersnap cookies flowed from the kitchen. Mom had a mug and plate for each of us.

"Sit down, ladies," she told us. "Girls, as Carmen's mom, I'm very concerned about her friendships. I want her friends to be young ladies with good character, and I expect Carmen to demonstrate good qualities as well. I am not trying to take over this sleepover and tell you guys what to do, but, Imani, I just spoke to your mom and we're on the same page. Riana and Layah, I've known you guys for a while now, and I know your parents well. You girls are expected to treat each other respectfully."

No one said a word. My mom was right. We were sixth graders. We knew better.

"So I just want to say to all four of you ladies, there will be absolutely no arguing in my home, or the slumber party will be over and you'll call your parents to pick you up. Even if it's the middle of the night. Now you all know that won't make any of your folks happy, and honestly I don't want to do that. You guys are sixth graders. You're in middle school now, and regardless of your differences or of how you feel about one another, you were invited here tonight to have a good time. From this moment on that's what's going to happen. Understood?"

We all just looked at each other as my mom instructed us to fix our tea however we liked. I cared about Layah and Riana, *and* I wanted to get to know Imani better. Why couldn't we do that without the drama?

"I hear you, Mrs. Browne, and I'm trying, but Carmen

has changed since we've been in middle school. She may not see it, but she has," Layah said.

"It's good to talk it out, Layah. Now is a perfect time for you guys to talk through all of that. Tell Carmen how you think she's let you down, and, Carmen, you tell them how you feel too. Girls, hear each other out. Don't just care about your own feelings. Put yourself in someone else's shoes and watch this rift begin to iron out. Trust me, you'll begin to realize that things aren't so messed up."

4
All That

The next morning after my friends were gone, there were two reasons why I felt really great. One, because they were gone, and two, because my mom and I were having mom and daughter alone time. She was taking me to the mall to get new clothes. She'd only bought me a few items when school started because she said funds were low. Now that she had gotten paid from all of her artwork, which she'd done throughout the summer, she said I could go and pick out a few more things.

In the car on the way to the mall she said, "I see you're smiling awfully wide, young lady. So after my talk with your friends, did you guys work everything out? No more arguing?"

"Hardly," I said. I looked out the window and smiled because we were getting closer to the mall.

"What do you mean, hardly? I didn't hear you all disagreeing."

"Well, we didn't really fuss anymore. But we didn't get along either. It was hard all night, Mom. Basically Riana and Layah couldn't take that I have a new friend. I've stopped trying to make them feel good about it. So we all fell asleep; then this morning we ate, and they couldn't pack fast enough. I was so ready for them to leave that I helped them pack. I think I like Imani though."

"Oh, you do? And why is that?"

I told my mom that Imani had a lot of good characteristics. For one, she seemed to care how I felt about things. Two, she liked a lot of the same things that I liked. Plus, maybe it was time for someone new. I didn't realize that I could feel as much for Riana and Layah a year ago as I did now. I'm glad I gave them a try, so I thought that maybe I would do the same for Imani.

"Well, those are all good reasons to like a friend. I know how much you care for Layah and Riana. I just don't want you to regret later that you put them off."

"It's not my fault, Mom," I cut in and said.

"I understand. I understand that you don't think it's your fault. I'm not blaming you or anything like that. Clay told me how popular you are in middle school. You've got a great personality. You remind me of myself when I was your age. I just don't want you to flaunt who you are."

I heard her. She understood me, but not totally. I wasn't trying to be a big shot and stuff. I was becoming popular, and I needed friends around me that could deal with that.

"But, Mom, I don't try to show off for people. I'm confident; I believe in me. If Riana and Layah can't deal with that, then fine. If they can't accept me for being Carmen Browne, then I have to move on."

My mother shook her head and took a deep breath. I knew she disagreed with what I'd said. So I sat there waiting for her to set me straight, though I did fully believe what I'd just told her.

We drove five minutes in silence, but when we got to the mall parking lot she turned toward me like I knew she would, and said, "Carmen, you have the Holy Spirit working inside you, and He doesn't want you to run from tough situations. He wants us to love people who sometimes seem unlovable. That's what Christians do."

I let out a silent sigh. I was a new believer and it was hard doing things God's way. God had to help me.

"Carmen, the friendship issues that you guys have will get better with God in the middle of your friendship circle. We have to involve God in every area of our lives. Never stop praying for them, no matter how difficult it becomes. Your desire should be to please God in all that you do. Understand what I'm saying, lady?" she said firmly.

I nodded, we hugged, and went into the mall. I found

a jean outfit with studs on the jacket and pants. It was off the chain, but my mom said it was too expensive, so I couldn't get it.

Thankfully, I found another cool outfit that was cheaper and looked similar. It wasn't as cute, but it was nice. It only had rhinestone studs on the pockets. My mom allowed me to get that one. I couldn't wait to save my money for the other outfit. I knew I'd look good in it—not to flaunt for anyone else—but for me. My mom was really proud that I said I wanted to save for the other outfit. She said that I was learning responsibility and becoming mature, because I didn't get upset about not being able to buy it right away.

I still had a long way to go in some areas, but I was growing. That was a good thing. I patted myself on the back. I was proud of me.

★

When I stepped inside the school building on Monday morning, I had it going on. I thought I got a ton of looks on the first day of school. Well, that was nothing compared to what I got when my rhinestones bling-blinged everywhere.

Spence walked over to me and asked, "Hey, can I walk you to class? You look nice today."

"Thanks, Spence. Sure, we can walk together," I said, smiling.

Now, not only did I look sharp, but I had a cute boy walking and talking with me. All eyes were really glued on us, and the weird part about it was that I loved the attention. What was happening to me? I was into the attention so much that I was only half-paying attention to Spence.

"What? What did you ask me?" I questioned, knowing he said something but totally unaware of what it was.

"Should I let you walk by yourself?" he asked, a little irritated.

"No, I'm sorry. I'm listening. What did you say?"

He gave me another chance and I blew it. Again, I didn't hear anything he said. I was focused on an eighth grader whom I saw walking by.

Deion stepped in between Spence and I and said, "Oooh, a cute sixth grader! You need to lose this lil' dude and give me some time."

My eyes naturally batted up and down. I didn't know how to respond. My heart raced, enjoying the whole scene though.

"She's not looking for a boyfriend, so step off. We were talking," Spence toughened up and said.

"Please, boy. I know you ain't challenging me around here. Any girl I want in this school is mine. I'm the defensive captain of the football team. Don't you know who I am, boy? I'm Deion Thomas."

"Are you related to Michael?" I asked, trying to cool things down.

"Yeah, that's my cousin. He moved though. What, did he try to holla at you too?"

Ugh, I thought, then shook my head quickly.

"We're just trying to get to class, c'mon, move," Spence said once again.

All of a sudden Deion pushed Spence to the ground. The next thing I knew Spence got up and rushed into Deion. He didn't move Deion back too far. But that didn't dishearten Spence. He looked like he was ready to rumble. And over what? Me? I didn't even know Deion. I liked that he thought I was cute, but what kind of attention was I attracting? This wasn't cool at all.

"Stop!" I yelled out.

I screamed a couple of times and Clay came rushing from out of nowhere, it seemed, and got between the two guys. Boy, was I happy to see my big brother. It was like all the kids in school were swarmed around us.

"Man, what's up?" Clay asked.

Deion took his index finger and jabbed Spence in the chest. "This young boy was trying to tell me that I can't talk to this sixth grader. What's up with him?"

Clay looked really weird then. "Man, you can't talk to that sixth grader! That's my sister! You crazy?"

"Oh, Clay, my bad! She's cute, and with your ugly self, y'all don't look nothin' alike. I didn't know. So this is the Miss Carmen I'm supposed to be looking out for?"

My protective brother said, "Yeah, you're supposed to be looking out for her, and you're causing her trouble."

"Do you approve of this knucklehead?" Deion asked, grabbing Spence by the collar.

"He's straight, D."

I overheard Deion lean over and say, "She looks kinda young anyway, man. I'll catch her in high school."

"Whatever D," Clay laughed and said. "You won't ever catch my sister."

Before he walked off, the two of them gave each other high fives. Something inside me felt weird. I didn't know what to do with these new feelings. I tried to dismiss them.

Deion apologized to me and said to Spence, "I like your game but don't come at me again like that. Take care of her."

Clay and Deion walked away. Before my brother left, he gave me a look that said, "You know he's crazy, so ignore Deion." I winked at Clay as a big thank-you.

I still felt strange about myself. I heard Deion say that I looked young. I wondered if he meant that I wasn't as developed as some of the older girls. I felt that I looked just fine a few moments before that comment. Now I wanted to go and hide.

I looked at Spence and abruptly said, "Thanks for walking me to class. I'll talk to you later."

I dashed away with real thoughts of insecurity. I'd never thought about wanting a slammin' body before. However, now it was all my little mind could think of. I didn't want to be the brunt of any joke.

Imani came up to me in class and said, "Wow! That's a cute outfit, Carmen."

I certainly didn't feel cute now. I smiled shyly and took my seat. Where had my joy gone?

✪

When I went home that day, I looked in the mirror at my chest. I was developing slowly, and it had never bothered me before. But now it was all I could think about. For the first time, I wanted my body to look different.

The ringing phone interrupted me. It was Imani asking me tons of questions about my outfit. At that point, who cared? I told her everything about where I got it, and even about the outfit that cost more that I hoped to get one day. It was not about how I looked on the outside; now it was about how I felt about myself on the inside.

"I'm sorry I'm asking so many questions," Imani said. "But you just looked so good. Everybody loved it. You've got it goin' on."

"Girl, please, not hardly."

"Carmen, can I ask you a question? Don't get mad."

"I won't be mad at you. What is it?"

"Why do you hang out with Riana and Layah? They don't have style like you. They're not cool at all."

I didn't know how to respond to what she said. It caught me off guard. My buddies . . . no style? Part of me wanted to be mad that she asked me that question, but I told her that I wouldn't flip out, so I kept my feelings under control.

"I don't know," I said, trying to think if I even agreed with her.

"You know I'm telling the truth, Carmen. It's true your girls have no style. Layah dresses like a boy and Riana dresses real country. But you, your stuff is tight. It just seems like you don't fit in with them."

When Imani and I hung up, she had me thinking. I wasn't mad at her, but I just wondered why she even asked me that. Now I was feeling even more weird. Emotionally and physically I had issues. Doing schoolwork was out of the question. So another day went by without me studying.

When I went to school the next day and saw Imani in the jean outfit that I was saving up my money to buy, I wanted to scream. She told me she wanted to be like me, but I didn't know she was that serious. Riana and Layah were on both sides of her. *Why are they with her?* I wondered. The three of them seemed real chummy.

I had no idea what was going on, but when they walked up to me, Imani saw the confusion on my face and she quickly said, "Don't hate 'cause I got the outfit you wanted. You know it looks good on me."

"You're working that outfit, girl!" Riana said to her.

Then Layah said something that really hurt me before they walked away. She said, "Yeah, Carmen thinks that she's the only one who wears cool, tight gear. She thinks she's all that!"

5
Damaged Smile

I was speechless. How was this happening? I hadn't been the best friend to Layah and Riana, but I hadn't talked about them behind their backs either.

Slick Imani said, "Come on, y'all."

Riana replied, "I thought we were always going to be friends. How could you dog us behind our backs, Carmen?"

Riana turned and walked away, not giving me a chance to explain. Again, I couldn't believe all this was happening.

Standing in the hall, watching Imani lead my two best friends away was hard to take. I wanted to run and tell them that I didn't say that they had no fashion sense, but my legs wouldn't move. In my heart I wanted to cry, but I was so stunned that no tears fell.

My face held the saddest look as I turned and walked by myself, for what seemed like the longest walk to class in my life. I was officially friendless. Me, Carmen Browne. Me, Miss Popularity. Why would Imani do this to me? Why would she go and get the outfit I told her I wanted? Why would she tell my friends that I said something negative about them when she was the one who said it? My heart felt broken in a million pieces. I had been betrayed.

Lord, I prayed silently as I walked step by step to my class, *"maybe I was feeling too good about myself. I was happy that I was a Christian and pumped that I had some of the coolest clothes in the school, and sort of happy that boys thought I was cute. But what did all that mean? It shouldn't be about me; it should be about You. And now You brought me back to reality, huh? I see that so clearly now. I didn't deserve Imani turning on me like that, but maybe You allowed her to do that so that I would be humble. And, Lord, I am. Nobody comes before You, not even me. I'm sorry.*

Though my eyes were open, my heart was speaking sincerely to God. I looked at people in the hall with a different view. I didn't look at them with an uppity feeling. I knew I was no better than anyone else.

So I continued praying. *Thanks for teaching me that. It's tough and my face doesn't look happy because deep inside I'm hurt. But I know that You can fix me. You can even fix Imani. You can fix what's wrong between Layah, Riana, and myself.*

52

*I'm stepping aside and letting You work. In Jesus' name.
Amen.*

Praying to God always made me feel better. It worked
this time as well. I wasn't all smiles or anything, but I
wasn't so down either. Why should I be? God was with
me and He could work anything out, even friendship
stuff. He had done it before. I had to trust Him to do it
again.

Thinking that way, by faith I did something I hadn't
done all day. I cracked a smile. I was glad to still have
God as a friend.

It was a chilly Wednesday night in October. Our
school was very excited to celebrate our homecoming
game. We had a winning team. Clay was part of that reason. He fit the role of a quarterback better than a hand in
a glove. He was a great runner and passer. Dad said that
he was a real team player because he made his teammates
better at their positions. The boy was bad.

My dad was so proud and cheered so loud that it was
kind of embarrassing. I knew I had to move away from
my parents. Cassie loved being with them. She was still in
little bitty elementary school. No big deal for her. But for
me, sometimes they cramped my style, so I asked my
mom for permission to walk around the stadium.

"Just be careful. It's the third quarter now, and you

need to be back here ten minutes before the end of the game. Do you understand? I'm not going to be looking for you, Carmen Browne."

"Yes, ma'am," I told her with a wide smile from ear to ear, wishing she wouldn't call me by my first and last name.

When I first sat in the stands, I had hoped that Layah and Riana would come looking for me, but they didn't. I actually didn't even know if they were at the game. We still weren't talking, and though I had tried to let it not bother me, it still did. Instead of looking for them and wasting my time being embarrassed if they dissed me, I decided to look for Spence. When I found him, I stopped dead in my tracks. Miss Imani Bastien was chat, chat, chatting away.

What does she have to talk to him about? I wondered.

Then I studied Spence's face and he looked sort of upset at what she was telling him. What was she saying? I walked down a couple of extra steps near where they were sitting.

"Hey, Spence!" I yelled out, waving.

He looked at me with such a cold stare. His eyes weren't warm at all. He didn't say hi or bye; he just rolled his eyes and looked back at Imani, as she continued to talk his ear off.

"Spence?" I called out again.

He turned back and looked at me. I motioned for him to come to me, but he didn't.

All of a sudden, my brother threw a long pass, the fans cheered and stood on their feet, and my clear view of Spence was lost because of the crowd.

I immediately ran back to my parents. They were so thrilled for Clay. I was devastated because it seemed Imani turned all my friends against me. I couldn't imagine what she told Spence to make him mad at me, but whatever she said, it worked. He did not want to hear my side. That really stung—harder than if I'd walked into a beehive.

My mom looked back at me and said, "Oh my goodness, your brother just threw a touchdown pass. Why are you looking like that? What's wrong with you?"

I just looked up at the sky and thought, *Why should I be happy for anybody right now, Lord? I asked You to help me and You're not answering. I can't fake a happy face.*

★

When I came home from school on Friday after such a long draining week, being excited was the last thing on my mind. With my dad having a big homecoming game himself the next day, I was surprised when I saw his car in the driveway. When I walked into the house through the garage, I heard what sounded like my mother crying. I peeked around the corner and saw my dad consoling her.

I was the only kid home and my bus was kind of early, so they weren't expecting me then. Clay was at football practice and Cassie was at gymnastics.

What was going on with my mom? I wondered. *Why is she crying so?*

Whatever it was, it couldn't be good. Her body told me she was in pain. She was holding her stomach like she had the worst ache of her life. I was so confused.

Did someone die? I thought. *Is it one of my grandparents? Are my aunt and uncle fighting again? My brother didn't get hurt at football practice, did he? What in the world is going on?*

I needed to know something because the thoughts that went through my head were too awful to bear. I couldn't move.

My dad said, "You're gonna be okay. You're not gonna die. You're not even sure if it's breast cancer, honey."

In a frail voice, she responded, "I know, baby, but this lump, it's just strange. I've got a bad feeling about this. Just when things were working out. I mean, things are going well with your career. Clay's doing well. The girls are happy. My sister and her husband are getting along great. Financially we are doing better than we have in years. And my art career is finally taking off, and now a lump. Charles, why?"

"Where's your faith, honey? Don't panic. We've got to be strong for each other and for the kids. The doctor told us not to worry."

I suddenly started to feel dizzy and hot all over. The room seemed to spin around me, and I felt myself losing my balance.

My dad approached me and said very calmly, "Carmen."

"Oh, honey, she heard us," my mom said.

"Carmen, are you okay?" my dad asked.

Hearing the news I'd just heard, how could I be okay? All of this was too much.

Lord, I thought, *what are You doing up there? Losing my friends is one thing, but losing my mom? No way.*

With that unbearable thought, I felt it would forever give me a damaged smile.

6
Not Good

My mother and I huddled together on the floor and cried in each other's arms. Though the embrace felt physically comforting, emotionally I was a basket case. The thought of losing my mother was too much.

Before I could let go, I prayed, *Lord, let my mom be okay. In Jesus' name. Amen.*

The word *amen* came out loudly and my mom was startled.

She slightly pulled away and asked, "Carmen, were you praying for me?"

No other words would come out of my mouth. I tried to speak. I tried to let her know how concerned I was for her health. However, I couldn't say anything. I just nodded my head and then buried it back into her chest for more tears to come out.

My dad helped us both get up from the floor onto the couch. My parents explained Mom's situation. During one of her regular self examinations, she found a small knot on her left side. At first she didn't make a big deal about it, but the next morning she checked again, and it had grown. She visited her doctor, and took a mammogram—a test used to detect breast cancer—and it showed abnormal tissue. She was told that a sample of the lump would be surgically removed to determine if it was a cancerous mass or not.

"Mom! It sounds like so much. And you're scared. I know you're scared, Mom, because when I walked in you were crying "

Dad started to get emotional too. Finally he broke down. He couldn't just brush all this information under the rug like it was no big deal, hoping that it would all go away. If it was cancer, what were we going to do?

My dad scratched his head as he looked out into our backyard. Who would take care of him? Clay, Cassie, and I needed our mother. My mom *had* to be okay.

"God, what are You doing up there?" I asked out loud again.

All of a sudden my parents realized that they couldn't show that much emotion in front of me. They both held my hands. Squeezing my palms so hard wasn't enough to make me feel better. I needed more reassurance.

"Sweetie, I'm going to be okay. God knows what He's doing. Yes, I'm sad and I'm a little upset. This is a lot to take in, but I have complete faith in God. Whatever He decides is best for all of us."

My eyes just naturally rolled to the top of my head. I believed in God as well, but I really felt He only knew what He was doing if He made her well.

"Young lady, don't roll your eyes," my dad said sternly.

"I'm not rolling my eyes at her, Dad. I want Mom to be honest and tell me the truth. I'm a big girl. I'm in middle school now. If she has cancer, that's definitely not a good thing. I know. Layah's grandmother has it. Mom could die! Since I've become a Christian, every time I turn around there is something stealing my joy."

I dashed up to my room, threw myself on the bed, buried my face in a pillow, and cried some more. I do not know how long I sobbed alone. The next thing I knew, my mother was in my room and it was dark outside.

"Sweetie, I brought you some pizza," she said as she stroked my hair.

I sat up and just looked at her. I loved her so much. I'd give anything for her to be better—all my clothes and all my friends.

"Dad and I just talked to your brother and sister about what's going on with me. Though they're sad and a little nervous, they're okay."

"How can they be okay when we don't know what's going to happen?"

"They're okay with God, Carmen. That's why I came to talk to you again. You've got to get to that place too, where you totally trust Him with everything. Even things you don't understand. When you wish it could be this way but God works it out that way, you've got to know that He knows what's best. You need to surrender it all to Him. I know it seems like things around you have been sort of spiraling out of control. So I want to pray with you. I want to pray for our family. God can balance the drama."

We held hands and she lifted up a sweet prayer to the Lord. During the prayer, I realized that I needed to surrender my troubles to God. Though I didn't feel great, I felt a little bit better. For me, that was enough to know that God was still there.

✪

Later in the week, I wished I were a groundhog that could go back into the ground after seeing my shadow. It was parent/teacher conference day. I had to sit and listen to my math teacher give my parents a bad report.

"Carmen is such a bright, capable young lady, but she began middle school as the social butterfly. She just needs to buckle down and refocus. As you can see from these notes from her other teachers, they've experienced similar problems with her. She's not working close to her potential. Her grades are nowhere near where they were in elementary school. Though middle school is a step up, I know Carmen can do better."

"Two Cs, two Ds, a B, and an F in English! That's your best subject. Carmen Browne, what is going on? Answer me, girl!" my dad said harshly.

What could I say? I wasn't adjusting well to middle school. I hated middle school. My grades would get better eventually.

Everything I thought of wouldn't be a good reply. So I just looked at my dad hoping he would cut me some slack, but of course he didn't.

"Answer me," he said in a louder tone. "What have you been doing?"

"Dad, with all that's going on with Mom, how could I study?"

My teacher didn't have a clue what we were talking about. She didn't pry, and I could tell by the puzzled look on her face that she was confused.

Mom explained the situation, and my teacher apologized and said, "Oh, I'm so sorry, Carmen. Now I know why you were distracted."

"Oh, don't let Carmen fool you," my dad said angrily. "She just found out about that this week. From this conference it seems her grades have been bad for a while. No more telephone for you."

"Fine, because I don't have any friends to talk to anyway," I said brashly.

"Good, because you won't be talking to anyone for a

month. And if you use that tone one more time, young lady, you'll regret it."

"The good news is that Carmen has some time to pull these grades up. She has the rest of the semester to bring her average up. Carmen, I can only give you what you deserve. You haven't even turned in a number of homework assignments."

I had to hold my head down at that point. All the stuff my teacher kept saying to my parents got me deeper and deeper in trouble. Again, if I were a groundhog, I would go deeper and deeper into the ground to never be seen again.

On the way home, my parents lectured me about the importance of starting middle school on the right foot. I knew that what they said was true. My head hadn't been in the books.

"Charles, calm down. She's going to get on track," my mom said as we pulled into our driveway.

"She'd better get on track," my father said, "and quick."

★

I'd been seeing Layah, Riana, and Imani all over the school the last few weeks. I was trying not to be so down about their new friendship. Even though I knew I shouldn't trust Imani anymore because she had single-handedly turned my friends against me, I wanted Layah and Riana to be happy. If they thought Imani was cool, then I could be their friend from a distance. I didn't want to be mad that the three of them had a friendship that excluded me.

When I saw them in the hall, I smiled, turned the corner, and went to my locker. I guessed they stopped walking because I heard Imani loudly talking about me.

Imani said, "Why in the world did she smile at us? Carmen Browne makes me sick."

Whatever Layah and Riana were thinking, they didn't say it out loud. Imani was doing all the talking. I was so tired of her fake ways.

I slammed my locker shut, went back around the corner, stepped up to Imani, and said, "Listen, chick, if you have something to say about me, I'm right here. Say whatever you have to say about me to my face. You told Layah and Riana that I said something about them that you actually said. Then you told Spence something that made him mad at me, because he won't talk to me. I've had it with you!"

A crowd gathered around us. I couldn't care less who was watching. I had to stop Imani from thinking she could control me.

"I'm not gonna be right around the corner and listen to you talk about me without saying a word. I'm standing right here, Imani Bastien. Anything you want to say, bring it on. No more lies—just tell the truth, if you know what that is!"

"Ooh," Layah said. "Carmen is mad."
Riana replied, "And that's not good."

7

An
A Plus

The thought of losing my mother to breast cancer made me realize that some things in life weren't all that important. Being upset about not having any friends was one of those things. I had God, and though I was questioning some of His decisions, deep down I knew He was the only real friend I could count on, and the only real friend I needed to be happy.

I had no problem letting Imani know what I thought about her. She pretended to be my friend. Even though I didn't know her that well, I let her in my world. She stabbed me in the back, and in front of her face I was excited to let her know that her actions weren't going to bother me anymore.

She stood in front of me with her mouth wide open, unable to say a word. She couldn't believe what I was saying. She knew she was wrong.

Riana and Layah's side chatter was annoying me as well, so I turned to them and said, "And you two, the two who were supposed to be my best friends, we vowed last summer not to let anything come between us in middle school, and now look. I don't know what this chick has told you guys that I said about y'all. You both should have known she was lying. Being friends with you guys isn't really that important to me anymore though. I might have done some things wrong, but I never tried to hurt you guys on purpose. Can you say the same?"

Just when Riana started to say something to me, I held my hand up so she knew that I wanted her to "talk to the hand." I wasn't trying to hear it. Something inside me finally clicked. I wasn't in middle school to make friends, to be popular, or to be liked. I was in middle school to concentrate on my studies. Since I hadn't been doing that, it was time for me to get on the right track.

Shaking my head at all three of them, I dashed off to class and sat attentively and took the best notes I had taken all year.

When school was out, I quickly called my mom. I asked her if she could come pick me up from school. She needed an explanation before she agreed to my request.

"What's going on, Carmen? Are you in trouble or something? Why don't you want to ride the bus?"

"I just want to talk to all of my teachers, Mom. I need to apologize. I want to see if I can do some extra-credit work. And I owe you an apology too. You've got so much going on, and here I am not doing well in school. I haven't been a good daughter, Mom. Forgive me, please."

She was silent for a few seconds, and then I heard her crying through the phone. It took her a few moments to answer, but finally she said, "Carmen, you're a great daughter, sweetie. I am so proud of you. I knew you would get focused about your work. I'll be there in about thirty minutes. I'll wait for you in the office. Go ahead and talk to your teachers."

"Thanks, Mom."

My English teacher, Mr. Randall, was sitting at his desk going through some papers when I approached him. "So extra credit, huh? That's basically what you're asking me for, Miss Carmen? I heard you were a great writer, and I was so looking forward to having you in my class, but you haven't been applying yourself. For extra credit you can write a paper before Christmas break. Since you've had such a long face in my class, I want a paper on your definition of perfect joy."

Mr. Randall was so tough on me. However, I was thankful for the chance to pull up my grade, so I would do whatever it took. I'd dug myself into this hole, and I was ready to climb out of it.

✪

Two weeks later we went to my school's last home football game of the season. My mom went to the concession stand and came back with her hands full. She sat down next to me and handed me my drink.

"I saw your two girlfriends at the concession stand."

I heard her, but I didn't care. I was perfectly happy and content where I was with my mom, dad, and Cassie. I took a sip of my Sprite.

She said proudly, "The A plus that you brought home was your third one this week. If you want to hang out with your friends, your dad and I are willing to lift your punishment a bit."

Layah and Riana had called me a few times. Though I couldn't talk to them on the phone, Cassie had given me their messages. Even when I saw them at school, I just kept going. I had no motivation on the inside to work on the friendship thing. I didn't want anything to get in the way of how my grades were improving.

"I'm okay, Mom. I want to be right here with you."

I had been clinging to my mother a lot lately. I cherished every minute with her. She was doing all this testing stuff with her doctor. We were waiting for the results. The waiting was the difficult part.

The game was quiet until Clay threw a fifty-seven yard pass to the receiver. The crowd went wild, including my father. On the next play, Clay got the ball into the end zone, running it himself. This time my mom lost it. My parents were so proud of him. I was happy for Clay too, but something inside me held back.

Two days later on Friday night, we were seated in the audience at Virginia State's opening of the play, *The Wiz*. Though Cassie just played a munchkin and a crow, she was so good. She made the crowd laugh. My parents beamed with pride. They said Cassie stole the show. We went to dinner to celebrate her success. Clay gave Cassie a knuckle sandwich to her head. He was proud of her. They had a special bond. For me, I was happy for Cassie, but again, something was going on with me. I just stayed quiet.

I didn't really want to admit to myself that I was jealous of my siblings, but deep down I knew that's what it was. They had talent. I felt as if I had nothing. I was so down on myself that I couldn't be excited for them. Basically I was envious.

I wanted to smile so badly and even though I couldn't, I prayed, *Lord, You've got to help me. I know You're the only One who can help me learn how to be happy in spite of what's going on with me. I know I've asked You for a lot of things before, but I want to be the best Carmen that I can be. You can't be proud of me, because I am not proud of myself. God, please help.*

As soon as I finished my prayer, I knew that I was headed in the right direction. Although everything that was going wrong was not instantly right, I knew that taking it to God was definitely the best thing to do.

❂

"I can't believe it's Thanksgiving," my grandfather said as he and I walked into church for Thanksgiving service.

My dad's parents were the only ones in town this year. My mom's mom, sister, and brother-in-law didn't make the trip. My mom didn't tell me why; I just knew they couldn't come down. My dad's parents weren't going to come, but since Dad had a special football game against the rival school Virginia Union, his parents decided to come and support him.

The whole month of November, my grades had dramatically improved. I wasn't going to be on the principal's list with all As, but I worked hard to turn things around. My friendship issues were still not solved, but I had asked God to make me a better person, and somehow I had to believe that He would.

Reverend Wright said during his message, "Your grass is green enough; be thankful. I said, your grass is green enough; be thankful." Reverend Wright repeated it as he got some amens from our congregation. "It's Thanksgiving morning and I know some of you can't wait to get home and eat that big turkey, dressing, macaroni and cheese, collard greens, and red velvet cake. Y'all know what I'm talking about. Peach cobbler, yeah, yeah. With that big meal, it seems easy for us to be thankful, but I've been counseling a whole lot of people this month who just don't seem to be satisfied with what God has given them. They are so preoccupied with what they don't have. They're actually jealous about what God has given others."

I thought, *It sounds as if he's talking directly to me!*

I was listening so attentively. I didn't want to miss a point. I noticed my mother smiling at me. I smiled back, wondering if she knew what I was thinking.

Pastor Wright added, "When you give your best, pray and seek Him first; you are already on the right track. Yeah, you may not have all the things that you want, but if you start thinking about the things that He's done, you will begin to see that your grass is green enough. When you start taking care of your own grass, watering it and not worrying about what's going on with other people, you can have joy. We don't have to compete for God's attention. He loves all of His children."

Tears trickled down my face as I listened to the pastor speak. I had not been thankful for what God was doing for me. I was so caught up in things that I wanted for myself that I couldn't be excited about the things that God was doing for others. I felt bad about that.

As the tears streamed down my cheeks, I prayed silently, *Lord, I'm sorry. My grass is green enough. If I want greener grass, being mad at my friends or being jealous of my siblings won't make it prettier. If I want You to forgive me, then*

I need to forgive; and if I want You to bless me, then I need to be happy that You've blessed the people I love.

Later at the dinner table we all said what we were thankful for.

When it was my turn, with misty eyes I cleared my throat and said, "I'm thankful that I have a family that loves me unconditionally."

"Go on now, child, talk!" my grandmother said.

"Well, middle school has been sort of tough for me. I've been trying to fit in and trying to please people, and I have messed up a lot along the way," I told my family.

"Basically I learned today that I hadn't been really happy over the last couple of months, because I wanted someone else's grass, but I don't have to want their grass to be mine. Now I can be happy for Clay, because he worked very hard at football and he's very good. Even though I can't throw a pass like he can, I can share in his joy. I don't have to be sad that Cassie gets applause. I share that with her because that's my baby sister, and she's a good actress. I don't have to be mad at my friends because they listened to some lies and believed someone else over me."

I continued, "I shouldn't be bitter and not forgive my friends when I want God to forgive me. I don't have to be angry with God when I don't think that He answers my prayers and when I think that He might take someone very precious away from me. I need to trust that God knows what He's doing."

My mother couldn't hold back her tears at that point, because she knew that I was talking about her.

"I keep wanting God to give me more, but He's already given me so much. And knowing how blessed I am today, I'm so thankful. I'm thankful for my family. I'm thankful God showed me how to truly have joy. I'm also thankful for this great meal that I can't wait to eat," I said as I licked my lips at the delicious-looking spread before me.

My grandfather said, "Carmen Browne, when we were walking into church today you looked a little sad. I prayed God would speak to your heart. You're too young to look so stressed out. Looks like God answered your prayers and mine. You've made me so proud. If I were your teacher, girl, for that speech you'd get an A plus."

8

Coming Together

A week later, I went to school and walked straight up to Riana and Layah. The two of them were standing together by their lockers. Though mine was just around the corner, I had avoided going when I didn't have to in the past few weeks. However, today was different.

I pulled out two fuchsia envelopes. One was addressed, "To my cool friend Layah." The other, "To my sweet friend Riana."

The invitation read:

You are cordially invited to attend a Friendship Reconciliation Tea. Saturday, December the 7th 11 AM–1 PM Theme: Working Through Our Differences.

After the two of them read it, they looked at each other. Their looks made me think they didn't want to come. My head dropped.

My mom and I had talked a lot over my Thanksgiving break about all of the friendship issues that I had. I told her how Imani helped to destroy my already-strained friendship with Layah and Riana. Mom said that I should be proactive about trying to heal our friendship. I asked her if I could have a tea for Riana and Layah, and she thought that would be a good idea. I gave out the invitations, and now it was up to Layah and Riana to accept or not.

After a long pause, to my surprise Riana said, "We would love to come. Thanks for inviting us."

She reached over and then squeezed my arm. Layah smiled, gave me the thumbs-up, and told me that she couldn't wait to be there. Then the two of them walked away from their lockers, huddled, giggling about their invites. I couldn't help but smile. I missed my friends and it seemed as though they had missed me. This tea was going to be a new start for us.

Friday couldn't come fast enough. I had taken three tests on Thursday, and I was excited to see two As and a B. As I helped my mom set the table for the next day, Clay came into the dining room as my mother stepped into the kitchen.

"Hey, sis."

"Hey."

"I need to ask you something."

Lately, Clay had been so busy with school, football, and girls calling on the phone that I just knew I was the last person he would need to talk to. So when he came to ask me a question I put down the sterling silverware to listen.

"What do you want to ask me?"

"What's goin' on with you and Spence? I haven't seen you guys in school together at all lately. I ran into him to-day and asked him what was goin' on, and he said that he didn't want to talk about it."

"Aww, my big brother cares," I said, going up to him and pinching his cheeks.

"What's up? What'd you do to him?"

"Nothing!" I said defensively. "He was talking to this girl that I thought was my friend one day. He looked really mad and hasn't spoken to me since. That was a month ago. I'm not going to beg him to talk to me. If he believes what some girl said without talking to me about it, then he wasn't my friend anyway."

"That's really how you feel?" my brother asked.

I just shrugged my shoulders, knowing that there was nothing I could do about the situation.

"Well, I'm headed to the high school game with some of my boys. I'll see you tomorrow."

"Tomorrow? What kind of curfew do you have?"

"I'll be in tonight, but you'll be asleep."

"Boys get to have all the fun," I said, huffing.

He teased by saying, "Remember Reverend Wright's words—don't hate."

"You're right. I'm just playing," I said, giving Clay a quick good-bye hug.

★

When I woke up the next morning I was so pumped about my tea. I woke up at six in the morning and walked past Clay's room and heard him snoring. Cassie was still asleep as well. My parents were even still sleeping. My dad had an off week before Virginia State's big championship game. His Trojans were doing so well. They had only lost one game and next week were set to play Bowie State in Richmond. That was natural territory for both teams.

Finally, it was ten o'clock. My brother, sister, and dad were all gone to spend the day together. Mom was in the kitchen baking a quiche that smelled so good. She let me help bake the strawberry cheesecake muffins and the red velvet cupcakes. The menu also included crab dip with crackers and chicken lasagna.

The tea of choice was Earl Grey. My mother liked to serve it when she had her girlfriends over. I knew I would need a lot of honey and sugar to make it taste good. Since my mom served this kind of tea to her friends, serving it to my friends made me feel important.

Layah and Riana arrived right on time. My mom served us and then left us alone.

Before I could get into why I wanted them to come over so badly, Layah said, "Hey, Carmen, we owe you an apology. We took Imani's word over yours, and we believed that you were talking about us. We turned our backs on you when we should have turned our back on her. Do you forgive us?"

"Yeah, Carmen," Riana chimed in. "We're girls. You said it best in the hall that day, and even though we didn't want to admit it at the time, you made us think. We love you."

"I love y'all too. Y'all aren't the only ones who owe an apology here today. I owe you guys one too. I was so worried about being popular that I didn't even take time for my friends."

"Yeah, but we should have been happy for you," Layah said.

It was such a good time. The food was delicious and the fellowship was awesome. I had missed this.

As we sipped the Earl Grey tea that was actually quite tasty, I said, "Friendships, like the one that we have, should last forever. We can't ever stop talking to one another so that no drama can come between us. No one should be able to pull us apart."

They told me how boring their lives had been without me, and I confessed that I had been miserable without them too. Yep, I had great friends in Layah and Riana, and I thanked God that He allowed us to work things out. Mom always said that God works everything out for our good.

★

"Oh, boy," my mother said as we sat on the edge of the bleacher at my dad's championship game. "We're gonna lose!"

There were only two minutes left in the game, and we were down sixteen to thirteen. Though the game wasn't over yet, I had to agree with her. We weren't going to pull this one out. I searched the field to find my dad. He was pacing back and forth. I knew when he paced like that, it meant he wasn't too happy with his team. They had worked so hard, only losing one other game this season. I knew he was going to take this loss pretty hard since this was the championship game.

After I looked at my father, I noticed Clay talking to Spence on the sidelines. I didn't know what they were saying, but Clay pointed up toward me. Then when they saw me looking, Spence waved. Instinctively I waved back. Then a big smile appeared on his face. At that point I couldn't wait for the game to be over. There was no way we could win it anyway. I wanted to talk to Clay. I had to see what he was up to. As soon as the buzzer sounded, the team shook hands with the opponents, and I lost Clay and Spence in the crowd.

I was following my mother down to the locker room, but she kept stopping. Everyone wanted to tell her that it was okay that we lost and that we had a great season.

That was all fine and dandy, but I wanted to talk to my friend. All the interruptions really bothered me. Then I noticed that it helped my mother. She was sad for Dad and his Trojans. But her reaction to people who encouraged her by saying what a great coach Dad was and how he had a supportive family made me realize that talking to Spence or Clay could wait. She needed to hear that.

I must admit, however, that when we made it through the crowd to the locker room, I was happy because I saw Spence just waiting around, almost as if he were waiting for me. He was just standing around with his hands in his pocket, kicking his feet as if he was kicking up dirt. He walked in my direction but also motioned for me to walk toward him. I guess he didn't want to talk in front of my mom and Cassie. I asked permission to speak with him and when my mom said yes, I met him halfway.

"I just want to apologize to you, Carmen."

"For what?" I asked, not able to look at him.

"Someone else told me that you didn't have time for me anymore, and that you wished I would just go away so that you could talk to the eighth graders. I believed it, but Clay set me straight. Will you forgive me, Carmen? Can I make it up to you?"

I just stood there, amazed at the fibs that Imani told.

"I was jealous that the upperclassmen had your attention. If I'd talked to you, instead of listening to someone who I didn't know, none of this would've happened. We're cool then, Carmen?"

"Yeah, Spence, we're real cool."

We said good-bye to each other, and Spence headed to board the bus that he rode. I wanted to ride the same one, but my family rode the team bus. I thought my dad would be angry with his players, but he wasn't. He stood up on that bus and gave a speech that made me proud to be his daughter.

He said, "Men, I know some of you guys were crying in the locker room because of some of the mistakes that you made. I made a couple of coaching mistakes that I wish I could take back myself. Life's not perfect; that's just how it goes. We had a really successful season. Because I was your new coach, a lot of people counted us out. But after the first few games, we proved that we were winners. We only lost one game this season, besides this one tonight. What we've done in the last two years since I've been your coach is learn to work together as a team."

The team seemed to hang on my dad's every word. He cared for his players, and I believe they felt the same about him.

He continued, "You guys play unselfishly. You don't get jealous when someone else does well. You play for the good of the team. We can only build on that and take that into next season. For those of you who are seniors and won't be back next season, I want you to take what you've learned on this football team into life beyond your college years. I'm the first one who's disappointed that we didn't win that game, but I can't express how proud I am of every member of this Trojan team. Lift up your heads. We may not be celebrating a victorious game, but we can celebrate a victorious season. We're family. We can celebrate the fact that we are there for each other. We can be happy despite the fact that we lost because we gave our best. Our opponents had better watch out, because the Trojans are coming back next season better, stronger, and more focused on our goal."

When my dad took his seat, every team member on the bus stood on his feet and cheered. My mom gave him a big hug. No, life wasn't always perfect, but looking around me, I knew that when you gave things to God, He makes it perfect enough.

❂

I was so surprised when Spence called and asked if we could go to the movies. My parents said that we could make a family outing of it and they would accompany us, even though Clay and Cassie would be at friends' houses. After the movies, we went to dinner.

Spence was so nervous, but my dad broke the ice by saying, "Son, it's okay. You can speak to my daughter."

Spence just gulped down some water.

I thought Spence was really cool. I liked him a lot. For a boy he was sweet, kind, and shy too.

As we dropped Spence off and he waved good night, I thought about all the great things God was doing in my life. Yeah, middle school had started off a little rocky, but through prayer, God had helped me get things back on track. My grades were improving, my two best friends were back in my life, my dad had a great football season, and my mom was looking at life positively. Because she was happy, I wasn't as worried about our future as I had been before. Yep, things for Carmen Browne were really coming together.

9

Full Heart

"Look at Miss Goody Two-shoes sitting in the corner eating all by herself," I heard girls joke about Imani as she sat in the cafeteria eating all alone.

Layah, Riana, and I were passing by when Layah said, "That's good for her. That's what she gets for messing up our friendship. She needs to be alone."

"For real," Riana said as we walked to another table.

I didn't feel right about what was happening. I just couldn't leave Imani there to be embarrassed by those girls. Even though I knew a lot of people, I didn't know them because our middle school was made up of kids from several elementary schools. The way they were badgering Imani seemed really cruel.

I said to Layah and Riana, "Yeah, she messed up our friendship and she didn't know how to be a friend. Let's hush these girls up and show them that she does have friends who care. Maybe we can show Imani what real friendship is all about. That's what we did for each other. Maybe we could do the same for her."

I didn't even wait for them to give me an answer. I knew deep down they had big hearts too. I walked over to Imani and set out to make God proud by trying to do her right.

I put my tray down beside Imani and said, "Sorry that we're late."

Before I knew it, Layah and Riana chimed in, and the girls who were picking on Imani were very embarrassed. They couldn't believe she had friends. And cool ones at that. We made them step off.

Imani just cried. She could have rubbed it in the other girls' faces that she had friends, but she didn't. She was real humble.

She turned to me and said, "I owe you a big apology, Carmen. I wanted to be just like you. I was so resentful of you that you were cute, popular, and had good friends who would do anything for you. You had a guy who liked you. I mean you're in the sixth grade, you had a guy who thought you were cool. You had a big brother who took up for you. I saw you with a beautiful mom and a cool dad. I just live with my mom. I have no friends, and I just wanted to mess up everything you had and that wasn't right. I'm sorry."

I handed her a napkin for her to wipe her tears away, "Imani, I'm a Christian. I might not have acted like one all semester, but I'm supposed to treat you like God treats me."

Imani reached over and hugged me. Layah and Riana just smiled. They weren't bummed out or jealous that Imani said nice words to me. They were just happy that we all could get along. We had all grown since beginning sixth grade. We finally understood that joy couldn't be achieved out of envy. Releasing the bitterness that I felt toward Imani felt really good as well. I now had nothing inside of me that I knew God wouldn't be pleased with. I felt like I could hear Him better and please Him more. As soon as I got home that day He actually confirmed what I was thinking when He blessed me with a gift from my parents.

Dad sat me down and said, "Listen, you know I believe in rewarding people when they do well. You turned things around, Carmen. Your mom and I are very proud of you for that. You've had a lot of things thrown at you these last few months. At first you weren't managing them all well, but you've made us proud of our oldest daughter. Your teachers indicated that academically you're back on track."

"Yes!" I screamed, throwing my hands up in the air.

I knew I had been doing well but just hearing my dad say that he was proud of me made me feel really good.

"What's the reward, what's the reward?" I sang out.

"That is the reward," my dad said. "We're proud of you."

"Ha, ha," I said, holding my hand out for some money.

He slapped it and said, "We can't give you cash when we're paying for all these lessons."

"Huh?" I said looking real puzzled. *What had my parents done?* I wondered.

"Carmen, you know I love the arts. I'm a painter. Being creative is your passion as well. You love music. So much so that if you could cut your own album today, you would," my mother said.

I nodded my head in agreement.

"But I didn't just become a good painter overnight."

"Mom, you're awesome."

"Well, thank you. But that didn't just happen. I studied the craft. So we've enrolled you in a program at Virginia State where you will learn how to play piano and guitar. You will also take voice lessons."

I jumped out of my chair and hugged them so tight that they looked like they were glued together.

"You guys are doing this for me?!"

"We believe in you. We just couldn't allow you to have extracurricular activities until you pulled those grades up. Now that you've accomplished that, maybe you'll be motivated to keep them up."

"I will, Daddy. Thank you guys."

I left the two of them, bursting with joy.

✪

When I came home from school the next day, I could tell that my mother had been crying. Her eyes were red and swollen.

She said to me in a somber voice, "Sweetie, the telephone is for you, and I need to speak to you afterward."

She kissed me on the cheek and handed me the phone.

Before I could say anything, I prayed silently, *Lord, it doesn't seem like good news with my mom. I don't know what all that means, but I am giving it to You. Please help, Lord.*

"Hello," I said with caution.

"Hey, niece of mine. What's up, girl? Does school have you drained?" my Auntie Chris asked enthusiastically.

"Hey," I said with a little more pep in my voice. I had missed talking to her. I thought about my Auntie Chris and Uncle Mark a lot. I hoped they were getting along, and from the sound of her voice, it seemed as if they were. It seemed as if God had answered my prayers, and that made me smile.

"How are you?" I asked her.

"Well, I've got to figure out a way to get you back here next summer."

"Uh, no, thank you," I replied, remembering what a crazy ordeal it was the last time I was up there. "Uncle

Mark doesn't want me back there. No matter what he says, I know it."

"I think he wants you to come back. I mean, after all, we're going to need somebody to babysit."

"What, babysit! You're having a baby?"

"Yes, we're three months pregnant. The baby is due in the summer. Things are going so well with me and your uncle. He really feels so bad about how things went when you were here. We are both really excited about the blessing God has given to us. Your mother was speechless, and I see that the cat's got your tongue too."

I was really quiet because I couldn't figure out why my mom was in tears. *Is she so excited that she can't take it? No, she must've gotten her test results. Why am I thinking negative thoughts at a time like this?*

"Auntie, I'm so happy for you. You're going to be a great mom. If you need any names, I could tell you all the names of my friends."

"Yes, I can't wait for you to help me name the baby. But, of course, we don't know if it's a boy or a girl. Just as long as the baby is healthy, we don't care."

"I don't care either," I told her.

"Big hug through the phone, Miss Lady."

"Yeah, big hug through the phone," I replied.

I didn't even get a chance to hang up before the line beeped.

"Someone's calling me," I told my aunt.

"Okay, I know you just got home from school. Tell your mom I will call her later."

We said our good-byes and I immediately clicked over and said, "Hello?"

I didn't want to talk, but I had to because I had answered the phone. I wanted to go downstairs and see what was up with my mom.

It was Layah, screaming so loud that I couldn't even hear what she was saying.

"Girl, calm down. I can't hear you. What's wrong?"

Layah said, "Nothing is wrong. Everything is right. My grandmother is able to come home from the hospital. The chemotherapy is working, she isn't vomiting anymore, and her hair is growing back. Thank you, Carmen, for praying for her. She said she felt it and she's stronger. Girl, I just had to call and tell you. I have to go and call Riana now."

That was great news. Her grandmother was such a sweet lady, and I didn't like the fact that she was suffering so much. God was answering prayers. I always knew He could, but the fact that He was doing it made me more full than any glass of water that I could drink. With everything that had gone on with Layah and Riana, they didn't know that my mom had problems in that same area. I guess I wanted to wait until my mom got the results before I let my friends know what was going on. However, in the same way that Layah let me know that my prayers helped her grandmother, maybe I was wrong for not sharing. Maybe their prayers could have helped my mother. Because I didn't tell them anything, maybe my mom's prayers and my family's prayers weren't going to be enough.

What have I done? I thought.

I went to my room, laid my head down on my bed, and just cried. I was happy, sad, and scared all at the same time. I felt like I was about to bust.

My mother walked into the room and wrapped her arms around me and said, "Carmen, I've got some good news."

"I know, Mom. Auntie Chris is having a baby."

"Well, I know she told you that news herself, but I've got some good news that I want to share too."

I was bracing myself for the worst, but then I remembered that my mother said she had good news.

"Good news?"

"Good news." She nodded.

"You're okay?"

"Yes, sweetie. It was benign. It wasn't cancerous."

"Mom! Are you serious?"

"Yes, baby. God answered our prayers."

I looked up toward heaven and said, "Thank You." I knew then that it didn't matter whether I prayed alone or prayed with thousands of people. As long as I believed and had faith the size of a mustard seed, God would hear me through His Son Jesus.

"Carmen, He didn't have to make this right, the way we wanted it."

"I know, Mom. He chose to let you be here with us awhile longer."

"That's right, baby. We've got to make the most of our time. I wanted to start by letting you know how much I love you and how proud of you I am. I know you're about to go through a whole lot of changes. I even see your bust growing."

I just laughed.

"We may not always see eye-to-eye. You may sometimes think that I am too old to talk to about some things, but no. As your mom I hope you feel that you can come to me with anything. You got it?"

"Yes, ma'am. I've got it."

We both cried happy tears. God was doing such great things for us. If He did one more thing for me I wouldn't be able to take it. Okay, well, maybe I would, but this was a lot. Loving God felt good. There was no better feeling than knowing that He loved me back.

Yes, Jesus loved me. Not only did I know because the Bible told me so, but now I knew because I felt it.

✪

It was the last day of school before Christmas break, and my teacher handed back the extra-credit paper that I had turned in a few days before. I had brought up my F to a B, but to put me over the edge, I wrote the paper. It wasn't as much of a challenge as I initially thought it would be. We had extra time, and my teacher asked me to read it.

"See, you guys need to understand that you have a lot of things to be thankful for. You come in here frowning all the time and mad at each other, and you don't know how good you have it. That's why I'm proud of this paper that Miss Browne wrote. She's going to read it, and maybe next semester everyone will come back better students. Out of all five of my classes, you guys are the best, but I know you can be better. Okay, Carmen, we're ready for you."

I didn't want to read it, but then I realized maybe my words could help someone else. Standing in front of my peers, I smiled. My soul felt great when people smiled back. I began.

I Now Know What Perfect Joy Is
by Carmen Browne

It's funny. I used to think that perfect joy was about getting something. Like when I was five and I lost my first tooth, I woke up so happy the next morning looking for money under my pillow.

When I started middle school, what I thought made me happy changed. Popularity was what I wanted. I wanted people to know my name and my face. When I got that, it wasn't all that I thought it would be, because it actually turned my friends off and no one was "feeling" Carmen Browne. It made me even more miserable. It's funny, because friends became jealous of me because they thought that I really had it "goin' on," and I was envious of my own brother and sister because of what I felt they had that I didn't have.

I had to take a look at me. I had to look deep inside and ask myself, What is perfect joy? You can't get joy from popularity because the focus is all about you. You can't have joy when you are envious or jealous of someone either because if your heart is full of envy and jealousy, joy can't fit in. Some of us are gifted athletically, some in acting or singing or a number of other ways. We should appreciate the gifts and talents that God has given us and appreciate how He's gifted others.

Yeah, having perfect joy isn't about getting at all. You experience it when you're content with who God made you to be. Then and only then will you have a full heart.

Everything is changing for ten-year-old Carmen Browne. Her
dad's new job means she is in a new town, with new people, and a
new school. As she enters fifth grade she's grateful for Riana, the
one friend she made over the summer. But her eyesight becomes
blurry, and Carmen's sense of what's important grows blurry too
as she shuns Riana for a shot at popularity. Life at home gets fuzzy
too when it's revealed that Carmen's older brother is adopted. It
takes a school assignment about affirmative action and a timely
visit from an old friend to help Carmen put life back into focus—
to help her see the real deal.

True Friends
ISBN: 0-8024-8172-8
ISBN-13: 978-0-8024-8172-6

Carmen Browne Series

Sweet Honesty

Stephanie Perry Moore

10-year old Carmen settles into her new home in Ettrick, Virginia. It's Christmas and Carmen has a problem. She's bored and her friends Rianna and Layah are bored too. Unfortunately, their boredom turns into conspiring against their parents to have a "free day" at the mall without them. This quickly turns into a lesson on honesty and how much better it is to tell the truth than to try and deceive people, especially their parents.

Sweet Honesty
ISBN: 0-8024-8168-X
ISBN-13: 978-0-8024-8168-9

They screamed by her home one Friday night and stopped in front of the Thomas's house down the street. What happened next started a chain of events that got Carmen's attention and taught her some hard lessons about domestic violence and how her own desire to be in charge can spin out of control.

Golden Spirit
ISBN: 0-8024-8169-8
ISBN-13: 978-0-8024-8169-6

The Negro National Anthem

Lift every voice and sing
Till earth and heaven ring,
Ring with the harmonies of Liberty;
Let our rejoicing rise
High as the listening skies,
Let it resound loud as the rolling sea.
Sing a song full of the faith that the dark past has taught us,
Sing a song full of the hope that the present has brought us,
Facing the rising sun of our new day begun
Let us march on till victory is won.

So begins the Black National Anthem, written by James Weldon Johnson in 1900. Lift Every Voice is the name of the joint imprint of The Institute for Black Family Development and Moody Publishers.

Our vision is to advance the cause of Christ through publishing African-American Christians who educate, edify, and disciple Christians in the church community through quality books written for African Americans.

Since 1988, the Institute for Black Family Development, a 501(c)(3) non-profit Christian organization, has been providing training and technical assistance for churches and Christian organizations. The Institute for Black Family Development's goal is to become a premier trainer in leadership development, management, and strategic planning for pastors, ministers, volunteers, executives, and key staff members of churches and Christian organizations. To learn more about The Institute for Black Family Development write us at:

15151 Faust
Detroit, Michigan 48223